FISH JAM

KYLIE HOWARTH

little bee books

For Beau & Jack

whose little hands helped create
the wonderful textures in this book.

little bee books
An imprint of Bonnier Publishing Group
853 Broadway, New York, New York 10003
Copyright © 2015 by Kylie Howarth.
First published in Australia by The Five Mile Press. This little bee books edition, 2015.
All rights reserved, including the right of reproduction in whole or in part in any form. LITTLE BEE
BOOKS is a trademark of Bonnier Publishing Group, and associated colophon is a trademark of Bonnier
Publishing Group.
Manufactured in China 0115 LEO
First Edition 2 4 6 8 10 9 7 5 3 1
Library of Congress Control Number: 2014957558
ISBN 978-1-4998-0098-2

www.littlebeebooks.com
www.bonnierpublishing.com

This is Jazz.

SCOOba-dooba-diddly-dooo

Nobody wanted to play with him.

Beep-bop-bubbly-booo

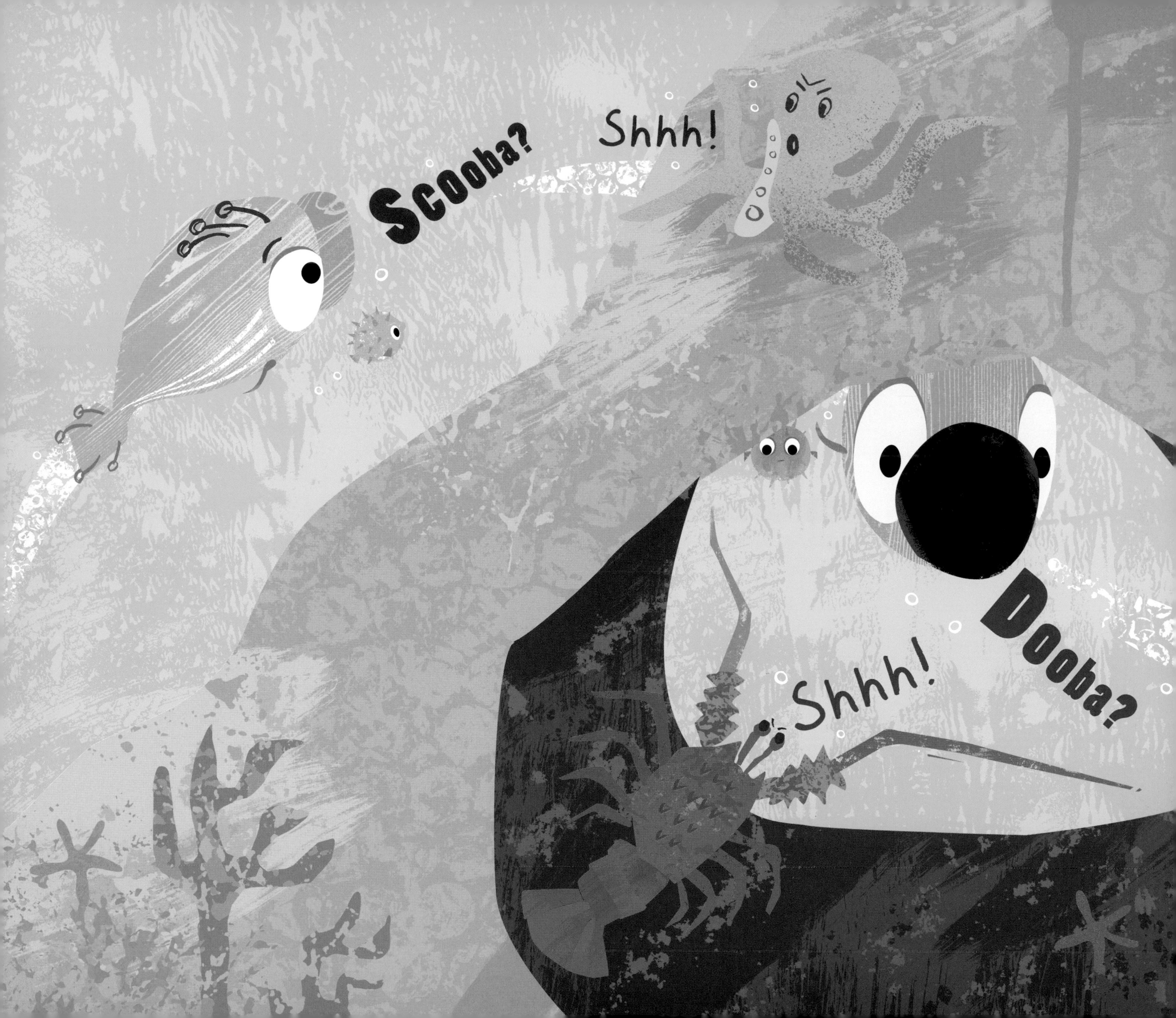
Scooba?
Shhh!
Dooba?
Shhh!

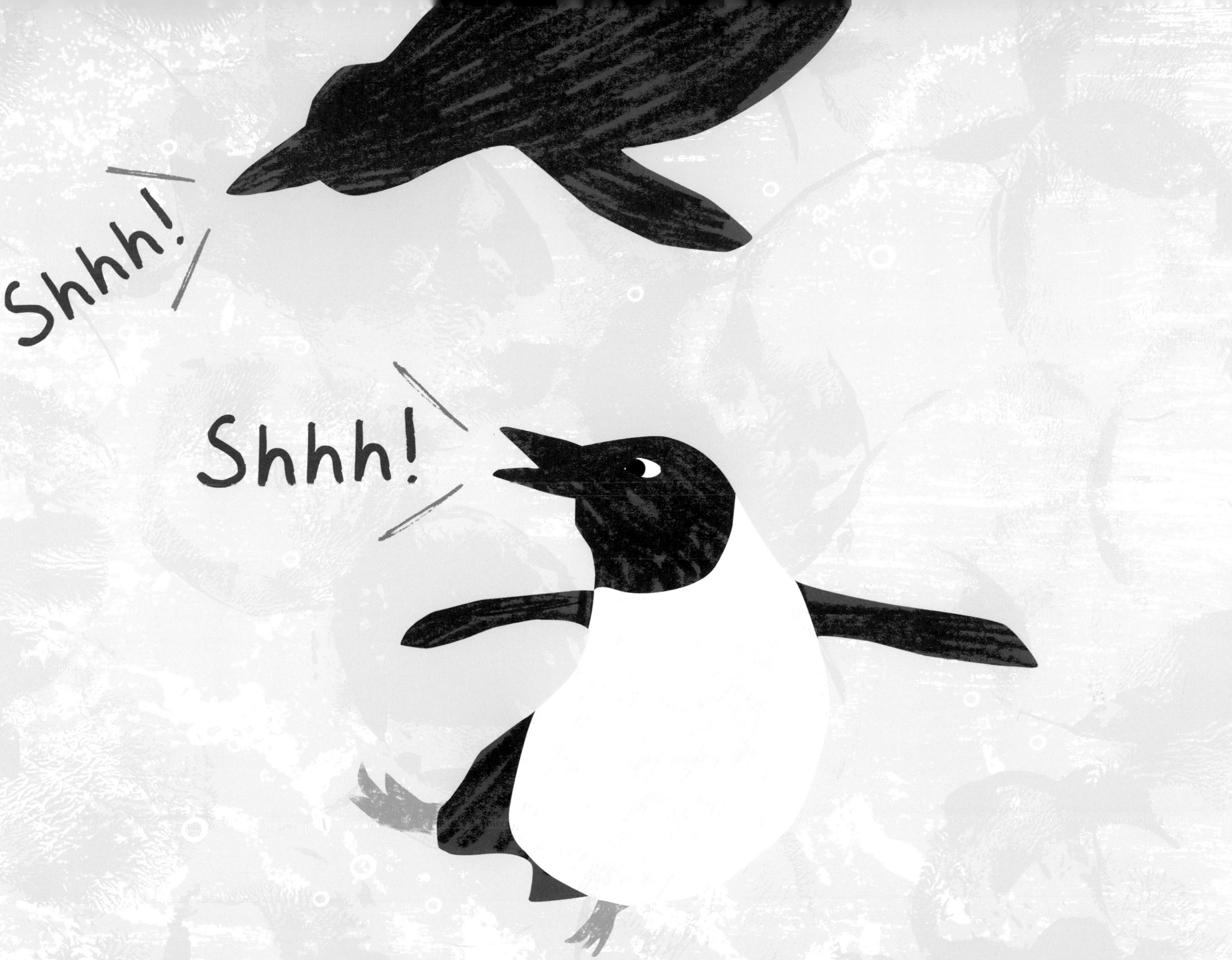

He was way too noisy.

Sigh

Beep?

Bop?

SHOO
SHOO
SHO

Until one day...

Doo - doo - doo - wahh

Doo - doo - doo . . .

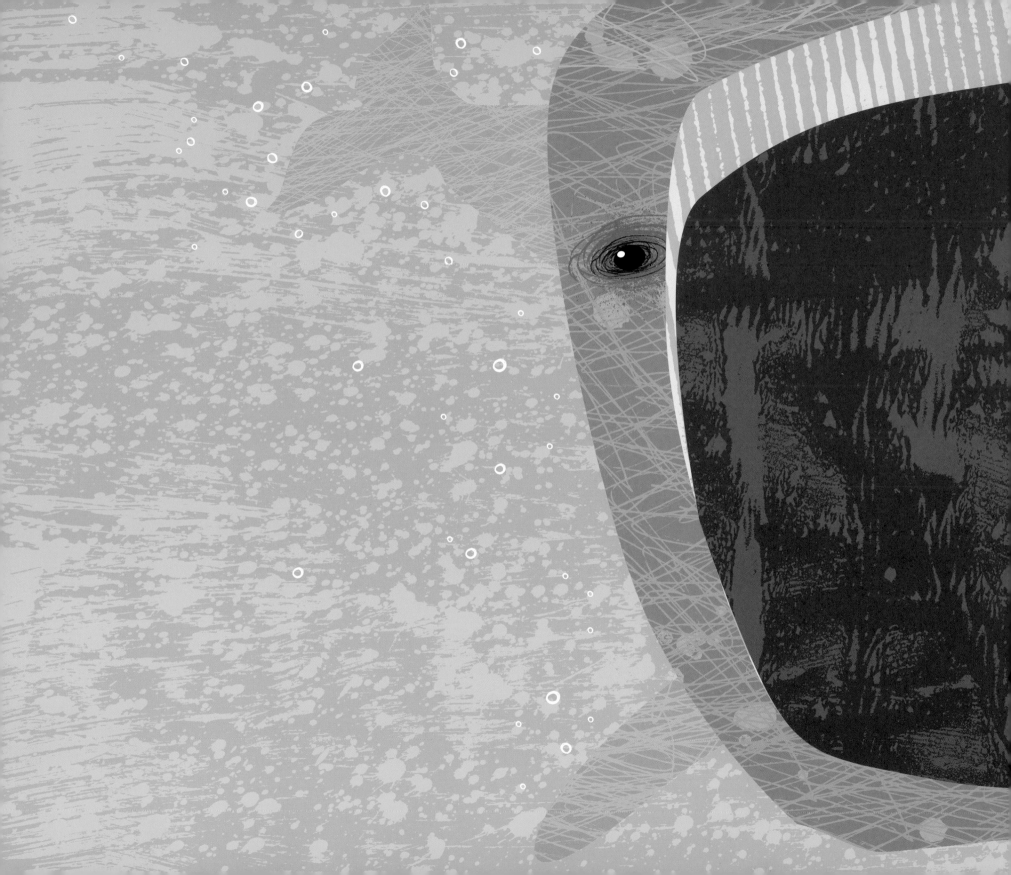

Something unexpected happened.

Clickety-click

Clickety-click

Scooba-dooba-diddly-dooo

Clickety-click

Clickety-click

Beep-bop-bubbly-booo

Clickety-click

Clickety-click

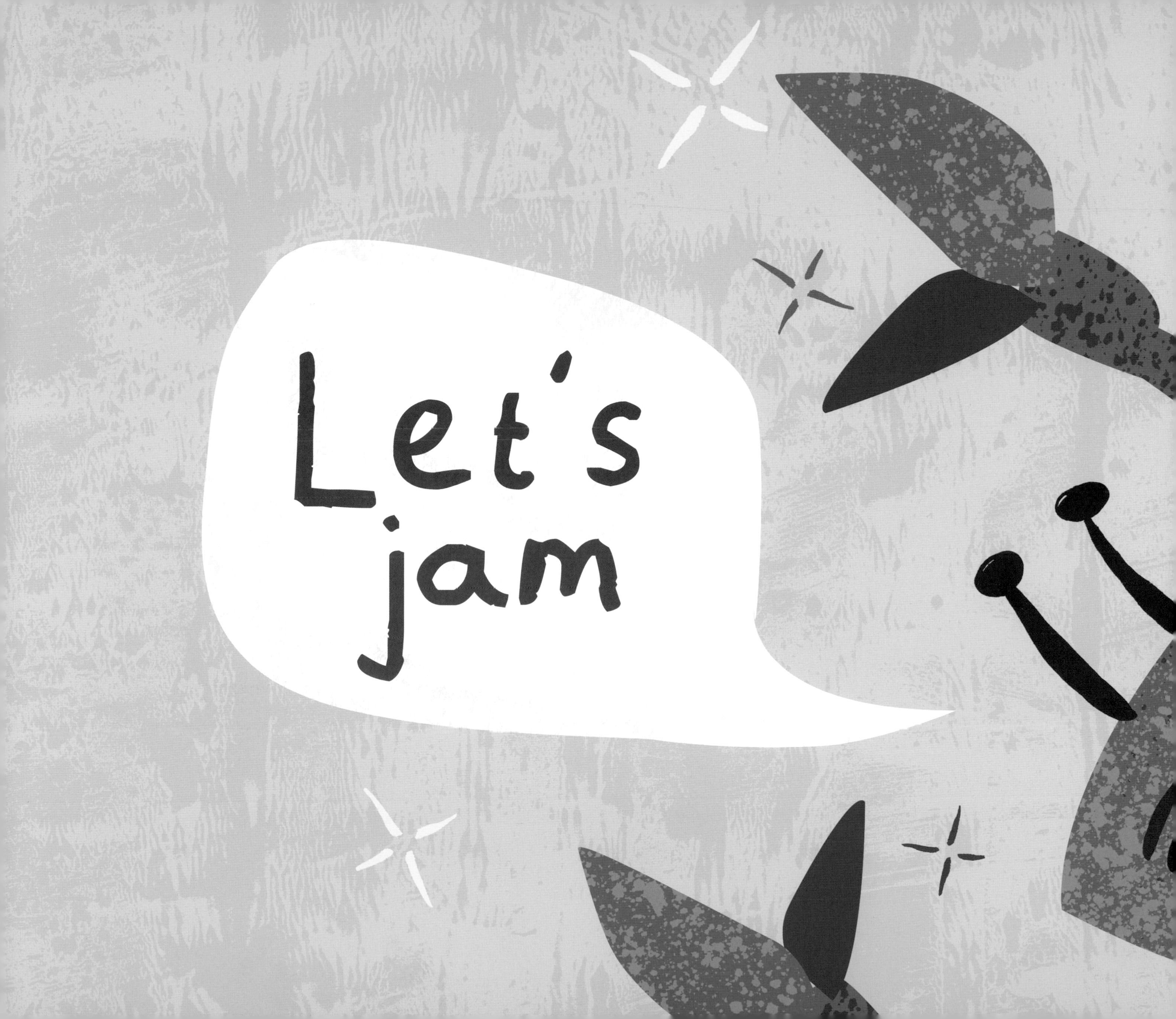
Let's jam

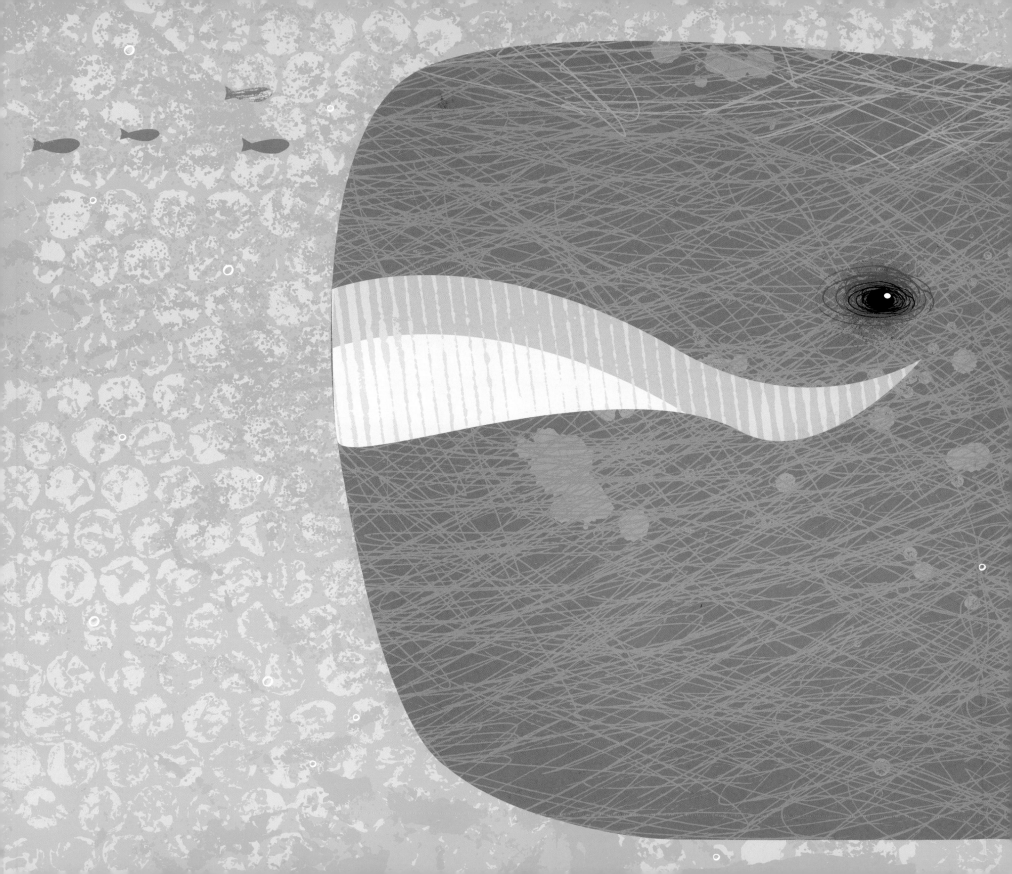

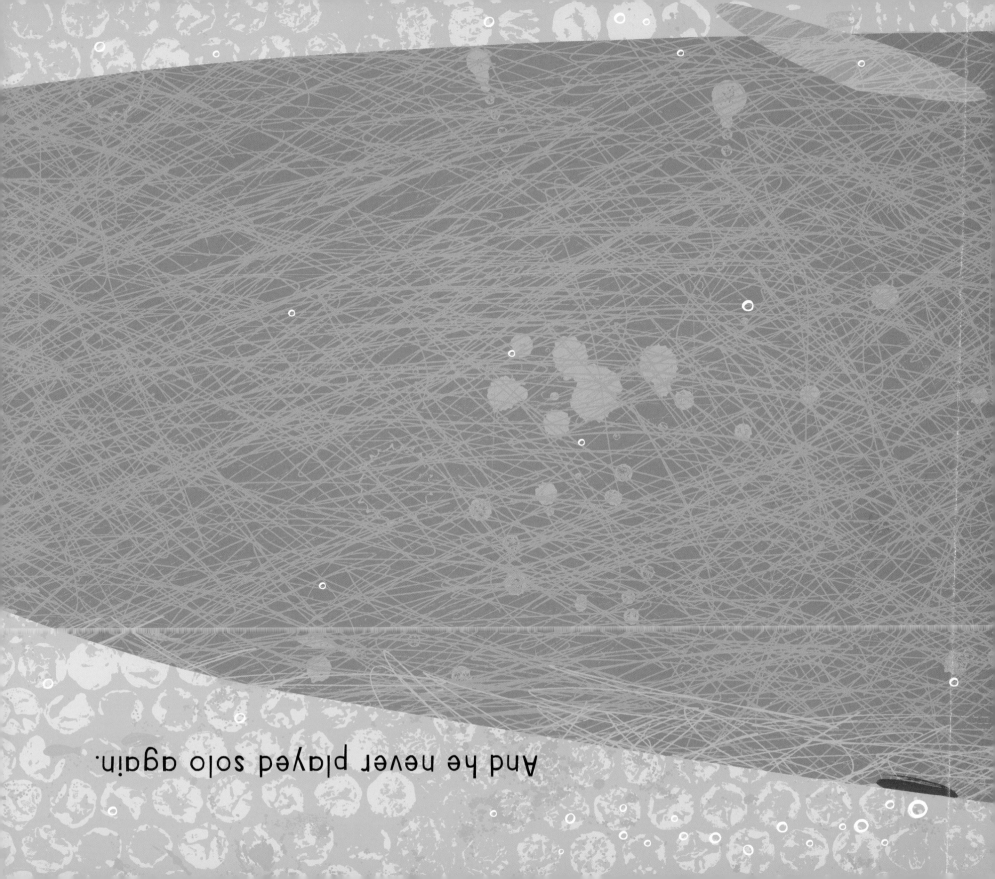

And he never played solo again.

That's the end of the tale.

Scat
is a popular
style of jazz
singing, where
nonsense
syllables are used
instead of words to sing
the melody of a song.

Use your voice
as an instrument!
Try making up your own
funny sounds to jazz up
your favorite songs.